CLIFFORD'S BIG RED TALES

Based on the Scholastic book series
"Clifford The Big Red Dog"
by Norman Bridwell
Scholastic Inc.

The Big Itch

The Big White Ghost

The Mystery of
the Kibble Crook

The Big Bad Cold

Scholastic Inc.
New York   Toronto   London   Auckland
Sydney   Mexico City   New Delhi   Hong Kong

One day Clifford had a big itch.

He scratched it against everything.

He scratched it against an apple tree.

"Clifford!" said Samuel and Ms. Lee.

He scratched it against a stoplight.

"Clifford!" said the bus driver.

He scratched it against Mr. Carson's truck.

"Clifford!" said Mr. Carson.

At home, Clifford scratched . . .

and scratched . . .

and scratched!

"If he keeps scratching," said
Emily Elizabeth's dad,
"he will have to go to the vet."
The vet? thought Clifford.
Clifford had never been to the
new vet before.

Clifford ran to the beach

and told his friends.

"Trust me," said Cleo,

"you do *not* want to go to the vet."

"What should I do?" asked Clifford.

"Stop scratching," said Cleo. "No

scratching—no vet!"

At the library, Clifford tried not

to scratch.

But he was *so* itchy!

He rolled over and over.

Ms. Lee looked out the window.

"Wow," she said.

"Clifford sure has a big itch."

"Clifford!" cried Emily.

"Are you scratching again?"

Clifford pretended to play.

So did Cleo and T-Bone.

"You were just playing?"

Emily Elizabeth asked.

"Woof!" they barked together.

Emily Elizabeth had lunch at Samuel's
Fish and Chips.

"How is Clifford's itch?" asked Samuel.

"I haven't seen him scratch all day," said
Emily Elizabeth.

They looked out at Clifford.

He looked happy.

And he *was* happy.

Cleo and T-Bone were scratching his back!

"That feels so good!" said Clifford.

But soon Cleo and T-Bone got tired of scratching.

Clifford's big itch got bigger and bigger!

Clifford ran down the beach.

He jumped into the water.

He rubbed his back on the ferry dock.

"Clifford!" cried Emily Elizabeth.

Clifford looked up.

"It's time to go to the vet," she said.

"Dr. Dihn will take care of you."

Clifford whined.

"It will be okay, " said Emily Elizabeth.

"You'll see."

The whole family drove to the vet.

"You must be Clifford!" said Dr. Dihn.

She checked his back.

"I have some cream that will fix that

rash," said Dr. Dihn.

"Poor Clifford. He's all alone

at the vet's office," said Cleo.

"He's not alone," said T-Bone.

"Emily Elizabeth is with him.

And she would never let anyone hurt him."

Dr. Dihn spread the cream on
Clifford's back.
Clifford felt all better.
He howled with joy.

Everyone cheered for Clifford.

Clifford wagged his tail.

He gave Dr. Dihn a big kiss.

"Oh, my!" she said.

"I think you've made a friend

for life!" Emily Elizabeth said.

"Dr. Dihn took good care of you," said

Emily Elizabeth.

"And I will always take good care of you.

Because you are Clifford, my Big Red Dog!"

Clifford THE BIG RED DOG®

THE BIG WHITE GHOST

Adapted by Gail Herman

From the television script "Boo!" by Lois Becker and Mark Stratton

Illustrated by Ken Edwards

**Based on the Scholastic book series
"Clifford The Big Red Dog"
by Norman Bridwell**

It was Halloween night

on Birdwell Island.

Everyone was going to the beach.

They were going to see

a spooky movie.

"Grrr!" A scary monster ran up to Clifford. Clifford backed away. Then he saw it was Mac.

"That was scary!" said Clifford.

"Nothing scares Jetta and me," Mac said.

"Not even T-Bone?" asked Cleo.

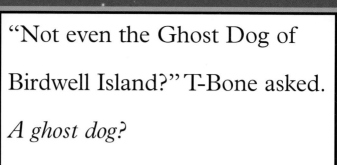

"Not even the Ghost Dog of Birdwell Island?" T-Bone asked.

A ghost dog?

Clifford's fur stood on end.

But Mac only laughed.

"There's no such thing as ghosts," he said.

The movie was about to begin.

Emily Elizabeth patted Clifford.

"He has never seen a movie,"

she told Jetta.

"And this is a spooky one!"

"Nothing scares us,"

Jetta said. "Right, Mac?"

A ghost appeared

on the movie screen.

Clifford gasped.

Jetta and Mac
yawned.

Clifford hid his eyes

for the whole movie.

Finally, he peeked out.

Emily Elizabeth was clapping.

The movie was over.

Everyone went back to town.

But Clifford stayed behind.

He wanted to know how all the

people got into the movie screen.

Clifford looked at the screen.

It was just a big white sheet.

The wind blew. *Whoosh!*

The sheet flapped.

The wind blew harder. *Whoosh!*

The sheet blew free.

It dropped over Clifford.

Clifford whirled around . . .

. . . and around.

What was going on?

Now he was very scared!

"That movie was fun,"

said Emily Elizabeth.

"And it was scary!"

"Humph!" said Jetta.

"It didn't scare me one bit!"

"But it's fun to be scared on

Halloween," said Emily Elizabeth.

"I've had enough of Halloween,"

said Jetta.

"Mac and I are going home."

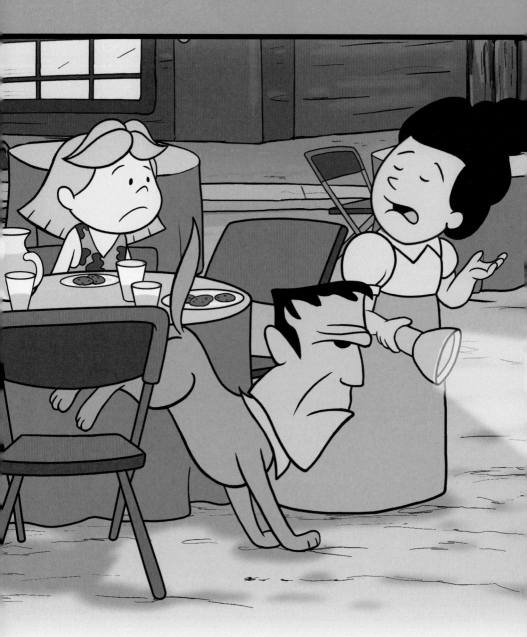

A few minutes later,

Jetta and Mac ran back.

"Help! There's a ghost!"

Jetta yelled. "Run!"

"It's big! It's white!

And it's coming this way!"

Jetta shouted.

Boom! Crash!

Something was out there.

And it was coming closer.

"It's the Ghost Dog

of Birdwell Island!"

Mac cried.

Everyone hid.

Only Emily Elizabeth stood still.

The big white ghost

came closer . . .

and closer. . . .

Emily Elizabeth stuck out

her foot.

The sheet covering Clifford

slid off.

"Why, it's not a big white

ghost," said T-Bone.

"It's a Big Red Dog!" Cleo said.

"It's okay," Emily Elizabeth told

Clifford. "I'm right here."

But where were Jetta and Mac?

They were hiding
under the table!
"Everyone gets
scared sometimes,"
Emily Elizabeth told Jetta.
"Even big brave dogs
like Mac and Clifford."

"Maybe next year, Clifford can wear a sheet for Halloween," Emily Elizabeth said.

"Then he will really be Clifford,

my big white ghost!"

Clifford wagged his tail.

That wasn't scary at all.

Clifford THE BIG RED DOG ®
THE MYSTERY OF THE KIBBLE CROOK

Adapted by Liz Mills

Illustrated by Gita Lloyd and Eric Binder

**Based on the Scholastic book series
"Clifford The Big Red Dog"
by Norman Bridwell**

From the television script "Kibble Crook"
by Dev Ross

One day, T-Bone ran into Cleo's yard.

"Clifford! Cleo! Let's play!"

he shouted.

But no one was there.

T-Bone lay down on the grass to wait.

Then he saw Cleo's bowl.

And he smelled something good.

"I'll ask Cleo if I can try

her dog food when she gets back,"

said T-Bone.

But the longer he waited,

the better the food smelled.

T-Bone thought he would

just have a little taste.

"Wow! This food is great!"

said T-Bone.

And he took another taste.

T-Bone ate more and more…

until it was all gone!

"Oh, no!" he cried.

"I ate all of Cleo's food!

She's going to be so mad!

What am I going to tell her?"

Then Clifford, Cleo, and Mac

walked into the yard.

"I want everyone to try

my new dog food," said Cleo.

"Oh, no!" she cried.

"What's wrong?" asked Clifford.

"Somebody ate my food!" she shouted.

"Maybe a kibble crook took it,"

said Mac. "That's what you call a dog

who eats another dog's food."

Cleo turned to T-Bone.

"Did you see anyone?" she asked.

T-Bone was afraid to tell the truth.

"I think I saw a dog run down the street," he said.

"Which way did he go?" Cleo asked.

"I think he ran toward the dock,"
T-Bone said.

"Let's go make him say he's sorry!"
said Mac.

The dogs ran off.

At the dock, the dogs sniffed right.

They sniffed left.

They looked high.

They looked low.

No kibble crook.

T-Bone stopped to scratch his ear.

"They are not going to find anything.

I'm the kibble crook," he thought sadly.

T-Bone scratched harder.

He bumped into a box next to him.

Then he heard a noise.

Bark! Bark! Bark!

It came from inside the box.

The other dogs ran over.

"That sounds like a dog to me!"
said Mac.

"Yeah," said Cleo, "and I bet it's
stuffed with my kibble!"

Clifford turned over the box with
his paw.

Lots of toy dogs were inside, barking.

"Well, Cleo, they're stuffed, but not
with your kibble!" said Clifford.

"Maybe we should give up.

It's only dog food," said T-Bone.

"That dog ate *my* kibble without

asking!" said Cleo.

"Oh, yeah," said T-Bone.

The dogs walked toward the
beach.

Mac stopped in front of a cave.

"Every crook needs a hideout,"
he said. "This cave is perfect!"

Clifford walked up to the cave.

"Hellooooo!" he shouted.

"Hellooooo!" came an echo.

"It's the kibble crook!"

whispered Cleo.

"Let's go catch him!" said Mac.

"Wait!" T-Bone said. "I don't think you should go in there."

"Why not?" asked Clifford.

"Because I'm the one who...who..."

T-Bone stopped.

He looked at the ground.

"What?" asked Mac.

"Because I'm the one who should go in there by myself," said T-Bone.

"That's very brave of you," said Clifford. "Are you sure you don't want us to come with you?"

T-Bone nodded sadly.

He walked into the cave.

After a while, Clifford started walking back and forth. "Clifford," asked Cleo, "will you stop doing that?"

"But I'm worried about T-Bone,"

said Clifford.

Inside the cave, T-Bone thought about
how he ate Cleo's new dog food.
He thought about how he told a lie to
his friends.

And then he walked out

of the cave.

"Did you catch him, T-Bone?" asked Cleo.

"There is no kibble crook. *I* ate your new dog food, Cleo," said T-Bone. "I'm sorry."

"Why didn't you say so before?" asked Cleo.

"I was afraid you'd be mad at me," said T-Bone. "But I promise to always tell the truth from now on."

Cleo smiled. "Okay. Let's see if there's more dog food at home!"

And the dogs ran off together.

Clifford THE BIG RED DOG ®

THE BIG BAD COLD

Adapted by Liz Mills from the
television script "Get Well" by Don Gilles
Illustrated by Carolyn Bracken & Ken Edwards

**Based on the Scholastic book series
"Clifford The Big Red Dog"
by Norman Bridwell**

Clifford was waiting for Emily Elizabeth.

T-Bone and Cleo were waiting with him.

They wanted her to come out and play.

Clifford looked in the window.

"Oh, Clifford," Emily Elizabeth said.

"I can't come out today.

I have a bad cold."

"AH-CHOO!"

"What was that?" asked T-Bone.

"Who was that?" asked Cleo.

"It's Emily Elizabeth," said Clifford.

"She's got a bad cold. Poor Emily."

"I know what will make her feel
better," said T-Bone.
"Get-well gifts!"

"We can make her a get-well card!"
Clifford said.

"We can give her a big balloon!" said Cleo.

"We can give her a bunch of flowers!"
T-Bone said.

"And I know just where to find some."

"These flowers are just right, T-Bone,"

said Clifford.

"Uh-oh. Stop, Clifford. Stop!" cried T-Bone.

All the flower tops floated away.

"Sorry," said Clifford.

"That's all right," said T-Bone.

"The flowers look different," Cleo said,

"but they're still pretty."

"Right!" Clifford said.

"Emily Elizabeth will like them."

"We still need a card and a balloon,"
said Cleo.

They walked over to the pier.

"Hey, look at that!" Cleo said.

Samuel was standing in front
of the Fish-and-Chips Shack.

"Free balloons today!" he called.

"Come and get your free balloon!"

Cleo ran to the balloons.

She tried to get one.

She jumped—and the next

thing she knew . . .

. . . she was floating up, up, and away!

Clifford and T-Bone ran after her.

At last, the balloons caught on a flagpole.

Clifford helped Cleo get down.

"How about just one balloon, Cleo?"
said Samuel.

Cleo barked.

"I'll take that as a 'yes,'" Samuel said.
He laughed and tied a yellow balloon
to Cleo's tail.

"I'm glad you're okay, Cleo," said Clifford.

"That's a great balloon!"

Just then, Clifford stepped on

something that was lying on the sidewalk.

"This piece of cardboard would be perfect

for Emily Elizabeth's card," he said.

"But look—I spoiled it!"

"Don't worry, Clifford," said Cleo.

"T-Bone and I will fix it up."

"This is like finger painting, but

I call it body painting!" said T-Bone.

"Looks great!" Cleo said.

"Just one more little spot, right here!"

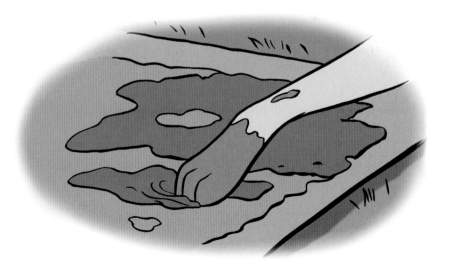

"Perfect!" said Clifford.

"Emily Elizabeth will love it!"

Suddenly, the wind blew the card

over the fence—

right into the Bleakmans' yard!

"Remember—the Bleakmans said we can't

go into their yard," Clifford said.

"Not even one paw."

"Then we'll have to get the card

some other way," said Cleo.

"Swing T-Bone one more time, Clifford,"

said Cleo.

"He just has to grab the card in his teeth.

You can do it, T-Bone!"

T-Bone went flying, back and forth.

Luckily, Mr. Bleakman didn't see him.

T-Bone went lower and lower.

"You've got it, T-Bone!" said Cleo.

"Yay, T-Bone!" Clifford cheered.

"You did it!"

At last, the dogs were ready

to give Emily Elizabeth her gifts.

"Are these for me?" Emily Elizabeth asked.

"Thank you all!

I feel better already!

I have the best friends in the world."

The Big Itch, ISBN 0-439-44943-X, Copyright © 2003 by Scholastic Entertainment Inc.;
The Big White Ghost, ISBN 0-439-41682-5, Copyright © 2003 by Scholastic Entertainment Inc.;
The Mystery of the Kibble Crook, ISBN 0-439-33248-6, Copyright © 2002 by Scholastic Entertainment Inc.;
The Big Bad Cold, ISBN 0-439-38989-5, Copyright © 2002 by Scholastic Entertainment Inc.;

12 11 10 9 8 7 6 5 4 3 2 1   10 11/0 1 2

Printed in Singapore 46
This edition created exclusively for Barnes & Noble, Inc.

2010 Barnes & Noble Books.
ISBN 978-1-4351-2426-4
First printing, March 2010